# UNDER A HOSTILE SKY

by Margaret Nash

Illustrated by Robin Lawrie

ANGLIA *young* BOOKS

# For my friends, Sheila and Jean

First published in 2004
by Anglia Young Books

Anglia Young Books is a division of
Mill Publishing
PO Box 120
Bangor
County Down
BT19 7BX

Illustrations by Robin Lawrie
Design by Adrian Baggett
Cover design by Andy Wilson

British Library Cataloguing-in-Publication Data

A catalogue record for this book is available from the British Library

ISBN 1 871173 98 1

Printed in Great Britain by Ashford Colour Press, Gosport, Hampshire

## Acknowledgements

The author and publishers would like to thank Dr Alan Scarth at
Merseyside Maritime Museum, the RSPCA, Alan Smith, Graham Cottrell,
Rosemary & Terry Warburton and Gilbert & Irene Pendleton.

# Author's note

During World War Two, Liverpool was the second most bombed British city after London. It was an obvious target as it was an important port that sent ships all over the world and received vital supplies from America.

This story is set in the Wirral, near Liverpool, in the summer and early autumn of 1940, at the start of the German bombing campaign against Merseyside. The Wirral, across the River Mersey from Liverpool, also suffered from the bombing. The bombing intensified from late November, causing enormous damage and heavy casualties. Over 4,000 people were killed on Merseyside during bombing raids from August 1940, when this story starts, to May 1941.

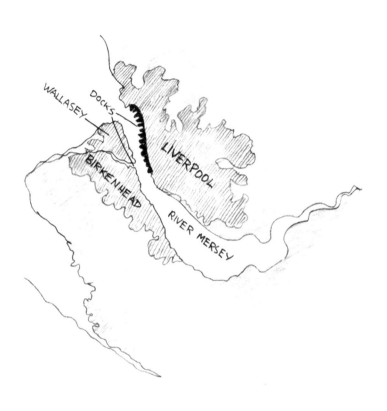

# CHAPTER 1

My name is Sheila Speechley. At the beginning of
the war, in 1939, Dad was in the navy and I lived
with Mam and my twelve-year-old brother Victor,
who was two years older than me. We lived on the
Wirral, in a modern house in Birkenhead. But one
night in August 1940 all that changed.

\*　　\*　　\*

I was deep asleep, dreaming of Dad, when the air-
raid siren went. I leapt out of bed and belted
downstairs in my pyjamas. Mam was hurrying
things together – bank books, a tin of toffees, a

flask of tea. Victor was peering under the blackout curtain.

'Heinkels, I think,' he said, although it was pretty dark out there. I knew Heinkels were German planes.

'Coat on, Sheila,' said Mam. I grabbed it from the door hook and slung it over my shoulders as Victor opened the door. Planes were already swarming in the night sky like a flock of dark ravens.

'NOW,' Victor said. 'RUN!'

'Quick,' said Mam. She took my hand and we fled down the garden to the shelter, slid through the canvas flaps and landed on our backsides. The feel and smell of damp earth hit me. I hated the shelter with its grey steel walls, all wavy like corrugated cardboard.

We could hear the drone of the planes and explosions of bombs in the distance. I peeped out of the tent flap and saw the searchlights weaving through the sky like long, thin fingers. The planes were coming nearer. I could see the black German cross on their wings. Then BOOM! The place shook and we were flung to the back of the shelter. Mam crawled up to the flap and looked out.

'NO!'

'CRIPES!' yelled Victor. Our house had its doors and windows blown out. Half our furniture lay scattered in the garden. There was dust and rubble everywhere.

'Stay here,' said Mam, grabbing our arms. 'The all-clear hasn't gone.' I huddled to her, feeling sick.

When the all-clear noise did go my legs were so shaky I could hardly walk, but Victor shot up the path.

'STOP!' someone shouted.

An ARP (Air-Raid Precautions) warden stretched his arm out in front of Victor.

'No way can you go up there, lad. You'll have to go to the rest centre.'

We stood in the blackness, in the middle of the chaos of shrieking neighbours, loose dogs, frantic air wardens and police.

'Anyone seen the family from number ten?' someone yelled. An ambulance burst onto the scene, took people on board and drove off into the night. A bomb had landed on the Co-op and flattened three houses with it. Ours was still standing but it was a terrible mess. I stared at

the grass littered with our belongings – the clock, lying with its glass front open, pieces of Mam's special china vase, and my muddy grey Wellingtons, one at each side of the path.

The next thing I remember was sitting on a bench in the rest centre, surrounded by dazed homeless people, crying like I'd never cried before. Someone was rubbing my back.

'Shock,' she was saying. 'You'll be all right, chuck.'

\*　　\*　　\*

We had to sleep and eat at the rest centre for weeks and weeks until one September day a lady told us there was an empty house for us. It was still in Birkenhead. It wasn't marvellous, she said, but it would do for the time being. It was a few miles away where the houses were more crowded together. But we had to go. You'd no choice where they put you.

'Ugh,' said Victor when the taxi dropped us off outside our new home. 'It's horrible. I hope they soon find us a better one.'

'It's a house,' said Mam. 'That's all that matters.' It stood in a row of blackened brick houses in a narrow cobbled back street, each one having a lav in a corner of its tiny yard. The windows had the ugly black tape criss-crossed over them, which houses had to keep the glass from shattering if a bomb fell near. We walked up the path to the house and stepped inside. Mam closed the door behind us and stood against it, looking into the dim room at the dusty rag rug over the stone floor.

'Right,' she said. 'This is it then. Best foot forward.' I sighed, thinking of our poor house not far away, cordoned off from the road, and the friends I'd left. I bit my lip and nodded.

There was a knock at the door. A lady about Mam's age stood there.

'I'm Doris Adams, love, from next door. I saw you coming so I've put the kettle on. Would you like to come over for a cuppa?'

We all followed Mrs Adams as she nipped over the railings between our two houses, and we were soon sitting drinking tea with her. She was cheerful and chatty.

'Eddie, my husband's at work, of course. He's on the docks, loading and unloading ships. And there's Billy and Jean.' She looked at the clock.

'They should be home from school about now, unless they're out playing.'

As she spoke, the door opened and a boy of about Victor's age came in.

'This is our Billy.'

Billy was tall, and stood with his shoulders well back. He looked very confident, and smiled at us all. 'Hello,' he said, then deftly cut a slice of bread and spread beef dripping on it. Between mouthfuls he told us he went round to Atkinson's the carter's after school, to help deliver goods by horse and cart.

'When I'm grown-up I'm going to work with the heavy horses on the docks,' he added. 'I think I'll be good at it.'

'Mad over horses he is,' said his mum. 'Always has been since a little 'un.'

'I like them too,' I said. 'So does Victor, don't you, Vic?'

Victor shrugged. 'They're all right.' I sighed. I couldn't believe his lack of interest. He'd been quiet and boring lately.

Billy looked up. 'I'll take you to see Toffee one day. He's the horse that pulls our cart.' He put his plate in the sink and picked up his coat. 'Mustn't be late,' he said, and he blew out of the house like a gust of wind.

'We must be going too,' said Mam. 'Thanks for the tea, Mrs Adams.'

'Oh, call me Doris, please.' She turned to me. 'I'm sorry you haven't met our Jean, love,' she said. 'She's about your age, I guess. How old are you, Sheila?'

'Ten.'

'I thought so. You'll be in the same class at school, I don't doubt.'

I went back, wondering what Jean was like, and if we'd get on. I missed my old friends. I hoped Jean and I would become pals.

# CHAPTER 2

As soon as we got back home Mam began unloading
the box of provisions the WVS (Women's Voluntary
Service) had brought. We had spam and cheese
sandwiches, listening to the end of *Children's Hour*
on the wireless, the bit where the presenter, Uncle
Mac, says, 'Goodnight, children everywhere.' It
always sounds so cosy.

'Ugh, this cheese tastes of soap,' said Victor.
He took a lump out of his sandwich. 'Look   it's all
cracked and hard, and there's hardly any butter on
the bread.'

'I wish you'd stop picking at your food and eat more,' said Mam. 'It's not easy with food being rationed, and people having to queue for ages at the shops just to get a small portion of meat or butter. And there's worse to come, probably.' She put the dirty pots in the sink and lifted the corner of the musty net curtain.

'Sheila, there's children playing out in the street. Why don't you go and join them while the sun's still out? There's a couple of girls skipping, and lads playing football.' But I was too shy. 'Victor will go with you, won't you, Vic?'

'No,' said Victor. He took his cigarette cards from his pocket, the ones with ships on, and spread them out on the table. They reminded me of Dad, who was somewhere in the world on a ship called the *Staffordshire*.

'I wish we'd hear from Dad,' I said.

'Me too,' said Victor. 'It's not fair. I know lots of kids whose dads are still at home, like Billy's. It's no different for them. Why's our dad had to go?'

Mam tried to explain again that, while the war was on, some men were needed in the jobs they were doing and some men were more useful in the forces.

Victor shuffled all his cigarette cards together, slammed them in the grey tin and jammed on the lid. 'It's still not fair.'

The six o'clock news came on the wireless. We heard the news so often I got fed up of it. I went upstairs to find the Billy Bunter book I'd brought with me.

'Oh no!' cried Mam. I rushed downstairs.

'What's up?'

'Shh!' Mam got mad if I talked during the news. 'Buckingham Palace has been bombed!'

'What?' I couldn't believe it. 'What about the king and queen? Were they in it?' Mam nodded. 'Are they alive?'

'Shush, Sheila. How can I hear with you going on? I missed that bit.' But I'd heard. The newsreader said that the queen now felt she had something in common with the homeless in the East End of London.

'Huh! I bet they don't have to go to a rest centre and sleep with loads of other folk,' said Victor. Mam didn't reply. She reached for the pile of clean bed linen the WVS lady had brought.

'I'll go make the beds,' she said.

'I'll help.' The blankets were grey, dull things.

I tucked them in well, wishing I still had my quilted butterfly eiderdown. Then I drew the blackout curtains.

'Draw them tight, Sheila, not a chink of light,' Mam said. 'You know Mrs Spinks got fined two shillings and sixpence when she forgot the upstairs ones.'

'I know. You've told me umpteen times.' I glanced down to the street. The children were gathered round the lamp-post now, chatting and laughing. I wished I could make myself join them. One of the girls saw me and pointed. They all turned and stared. I drew the curtain quickly, went downstairs and read my book until Mam made me have an early night ready for school next day. I hoped there'd be no bombs. I didn't fancy going down the cellar. It wasn't much better than the lav.

# CHAPTER 3

Victor went to the senior school like Billy. He set off on his own, but Mrs Adams had told Mam that Jean would call for me the first day. I waited for her at the back door, feeling nervous.

'Here she is,' said Mam, as we saw a girl in a brown coat come out of next-door's house. She climbed over the railings, her gas mask box swinging on her shoulder. She had brown hair like mine, but tied in bunches. She was smiling warmly.

'Hello! I'm Jean. Are you ready?'

'Yep. Thanks for calling for me.' I was ready.

I had my gas mask in its box over my arm and was wearing my name and address tag. I wished the fluttering in my stomach would stop. I wished I were going to my old school with all my friends, even though the teacher there was horrid. Nobody liked her. We'd nicknamed her Weasel Face because of her black beady eyes, which narrowed when she told you off. But what if this new teacher was worse?

'Good luck,' said Mam. 'And don't worry.'

We walked down the back street, into an alleyway.

'It stinks in here,' said Jean.

'Pooh!'

'It's called Pig Snicket,' she said, pinching her nose as we passed the pig bins. We looked up at a poster of a pig beside a dustbin labelled 'pig food'. The pig was winking. 'We want your kitchen waste,' read the poster. Jean made piggy noises at it. 'Grunt grunt, we haven't any waste so you'll have to go hungry,' she said.

'Don't you know there's a war on,' I said to the pig, then we ran as fast as we could, making grunting noises and laughing until we reached the main road.

'I'm glad you're in my class,' said Jean.

'Me too.'

We turned down a side street and there stood the school, a tall, severe building with high arched windows and the words BOYS' ENTRANCE and GIRLS' ENTRANCE engraved in the stonework over the two doors.

'It's not as bad as it looks,' said Jean.

The whistle blew and we lined up with the girls, then filed into the classrooms.

I stood beside the pointed easel until the teacher showed me an empty desk in front of Jean, and said I could sit there.

'Good-oh,' Jean whispered, as I slid into the seat ahead of her.

It was a huge class. Jean told me in a low voice that a few of the teachers had left to go to war, so some of the classes had joined together. Our teacher was called Miss Denton. Jean said she was OK, but added that Billy didn't like her much when he'd been in her class.

'Mam says he was always in bother for summat. He can be cheeky, our Billy, and bossy.' She shook her head. 'And a bloomin' show-off.'

Miss Denton called the register.

'Jimmy Wilson.'

'Not coming, Miss,' someone called out. ' 'E fell and broke 'is nose last night. He ...' The shriek of an air-raid siren cut into the conversation. Miss Denton stood up.

'Quickly and quietly, you know the rules. Line up at the door then follow me.' We hurried across the playground clutching our gas masks.

'I can't see any planes, Miss,' someone called, but no one stopped and seconds later we were down in the school shelter, piling onto benches. Miss Denton shut the door. The war was hotting up now, I felt. The boy next to me seemed nervous. He was sitting on his hands and kicking his legs backwards and forwards.

'I heard my dad telling someone that now the Germans have taken Holland, Belgium and France, we're next. Will we all be killed, Miss?'

'No of course not, Simon.'

'Where did Buckingham Palace get bombed, Miss?' someone chipped in.

'In the garden, mainly,' said Miss Denton, 'but one bomb fell on their chapel.'

'A good job they weren't in there praying, Miss.'

Miss Denton smiled. She opened the lid of an

old gramophone.

'Ow!' I looked down at my ankle. Simon didn't seem to know he'd kicked it. He was still fidgeting and looking worried. Miss Denton asked both of us if we were all right, then she wound up the gramophone. She took a package from her bag and gave it to Simon.

'We'll play pass the parcel.' The class cheered. 'Hitler won't scare us,' she said brightly, 'and he won't stop us having fun.' I couldn't imagine old Weasel Face at my last school doing that.

*   *   *

We came up the slope from the dim shelter, blinking in the daylight. We'd only been down there a short while. One of the boys dashed to the school gate.

'No bombs fallen, Miss,' he said. Miss Denton called him back.

'Come on, we've missed enough work time. I think it must have been a false alarm. But it was good practice for us.'

I decided I liked Miss Denton. I liked the bright red jumper she wore, with its string of beads, and her blonde hair that fell about her shoulders. I wished mine was like that instead of in great fat plaits. After dinner we threaded raffia through cardboard milk-bottle tops, which Miss Denton said we would use to make mats for Christmas presents, or for fundraising events for the war.

* * *

School ended with the same prayer we said at my old school, so I knew the words. *Lighten our darkness we beseech thee, Oh Lord ....* I thought of the darkness in our streets at night now, and hoped God would end the war soon.

Billy was waiting at the gates for us.

'Where's Victor?' I asked.

'Don't know,' he said, 'don't care.' It turned out that Billy and Victor had had a row. Billy said that Victor had cheated at a game of ollies (marbles). Victor, of course, said that he was no cheat and that was how the row began. But the fight had made Billy more determined than ever. He said that Victor owed him ollies.

'Shush,' said Jean. 'He's coming.' Victor ambled up to us, scowling, and Billy quickly walked on ahead by himself.

Mam was out in our back yard with Mrs Adams when we got home, and the rug from the back room was hanging on the clothes line. We helped her get it off.

'Your mam and me got it draped over our heads trying to move it,' said Mrs Adams.

'And nearly broke our necks,' added Mam, laughing. It was good to see Mam laughing for once. I'd not seen her laugh much since the bomb.

'It looks a lot brighter,' I said when we'd got it down over the stone floor.

'Well, I reckon we beat it within an inch of its life,' said Mam, jokingly.

'That rug will outlast us all,' said Mrs Adams, and we went silent, remembering the war.

Billy called over the railings. 'I'm off round to help with the deliveries, Mam.'

'Okay,' she replied. 'Ta-ra, love.'

'Ta-ra,' I called. Victor said nothing, and I saw Billy stare coldly at him. I could see trouble ahead between those two.

# CHAPTER 4

A few days later, after school, I was in the front room with Mam, who was sitting at her sewing machine. Since the war began she'd spent a lot of time altering and mending clothes for people who'd lost their homes. Hospitals, too, were always wanting second-hand clothing.

'We've all got to do our bit,' she said. It was a phrase she used a lot.

'But when will you make me my party dress?' I asked. 'You promised ages ago.'

'I will when I can, Sheila. Be patient.'

'I am,' I cried. 'I haven't had any new clothes

for ages and ages and ages!' I looked down at my old brown shoes, to where the stitching was going. 'Look!' I poked my finger into the seam.

'Stop it or I'll have you in wooden clogs next,' she laughed. 'How would you like that?'

Just then there was a knock at the door. It was Billy, with Jean standing behind him. He'd come to take me to the stables.

'Can my brother come with us?'

'I can't stop him, can I?' said Billy.

Mam came into the room. 'Why don't you go too, Victor?' she said. 'You like horses and it will do you good.' I'd told Mam that Victor had rowed with Billy, but I hadn't mentioned anything about Victor cheating. She unhooked his coat off the door. 'Go on.' And that was that. Victor came.

*     *     *

The stable yard was near the docks, about twenty minutes' walk away. Victor kept lagging behind, kicking stones along the pavement, with his hands in his pockets. Billy took no notice of him, but Jean and I kept waiting for him.

There were stables on three sides of the yard: a line of individual stables along a long wall, each with green doors and brass bolts, and then two large stables facing each other at either end. All the windows were blacked out because of the war. Billy said it wasn't a large stable yard. Many yards had more stables, but it looked big to me. It smelled nicely of horses and straw.

'Ah!' said Billy, sniffing loudly. 'Best smell in the world.' He told us the RSPCA officers often came to the stables to deal with horses that were injured by bombing raids. 'And we have a night watchman here every night, so the horses are cared for as well as they can be, really.'

'Do the horses get scared of the bombs?' I asked, stroking the long velvety nose of a white and grey horse.

'You bet they do! They hate it when the bombs light up the place. You've just got to calm them.'

'How?'

'Speak soothing words, use their pet name a lot, and stroke their noses – when you can. If you can get them near a calm horse, that helps. If it happens in the street you have to get them back here if possible, or if not tie them to the back of their cart. One of Atkinson's horses had to be shot because it went into a frenzy and broke its leg.'

'Look, here's Toffee.' Jean was patting the
nose of a beautiful brown horse with a white blaze
down its nose. 'You can put your arms around him
if you like. He loves people.' The horse snuffled
into my hand. As Victor and I were patting him
an old man approached us. He winked at Billy.

'This is Sam,' said Billy. 'He drives Toffee's
cart.' I looked at the old man's knobbly knuckles
and fingers, and was surprised he could work at all.

'Good condition, isn't he?' said Sam, nodding
towards Toffee. 'That's thanks to Billy here.' Billy
beamed.

Sam left, and Billy climbed the ladder to the hayloft and brought out a bale of hay.

'Catch, Victor,' he said, throwing the bale to the ground. Victor dropped it.

'Butterfingers,' said Billy, and laughed. He fished another bale out. 'Come on, have another go. Only *try* to catch it this time, will you?'

But Victor turned just as Billy dropped it. The bale landed on the stone floor with a thump, and dust and bits of hay flew into the air. Billy climbed down the ladder, turning to look at Victor and shaking his head.

'Nincompoop!'

'Bossy boots!'

'Dumbo!'

I didn't hear what Victor said next, but I heard Billy answer.

'Don't you say owt about my dad.'

I shook Victor's arm and yelled at him. 'What's up with you? Stop arguing.'

'What's up with YOU?' He kicked the bale on the floor. 'I'm going home,' he said, and stomped out of the building. I wanted to go after Victor and find out what he'd said about Billy's dad, but Jean tugged my sleeve.

'See that horse over there,' she said. 'He's called Duncan. He got shrapnel in his leg and had to have it splinted. He needs exercising now. You watch. Our Billy will start walking him round the yard. He'll be ages. Let's go down to the Woodside ferry and look over the Mersey, before it's dark.'

I could see Billy already making his way over to Duncan. 'OK!' I said.

*       *       *

We sat on the wall by the ferry terminal. It was like another world down there. The quays were lined with ships, so the water was never still and there seemed to be constant hooting and honking from the vessels. I remembered Miss Denton telling us how important the convoys of ships were now there was a war on, how they brought food from far-away places to us. On our right were the ship-building docks, with their huge half-built vessels standing proud. On the other side of the terminal were the pens, which often held imported sheep and cattle, although they were empty at the moment. Way down the docks, huge cranes swung in the air. Like long-necked dinosaurs they were, moving massive nets of goods on big hooks.

'Before the war the dockers were out of work quite a lot,' said Jean. 'Dad would go down there and often be turned away. But now there's plenty of work. They carry on even when the warehouses are on fire. Did you know that?'

I nodded. 'I wish we could go onto one of the docks,' I said, knowing there was no chance with the men and guard dogs at the closed gates.

Jean turned to look at me. 'It's great. You've to watch out though. The dockers all carry hooks to grab the sacks and netted goods, and the floors get slippy when it's wet. Everyone's rushing around too, and there are loads of horses, big 'uns. I'll ask my dad to take us sometime.'

We sat kicking our legs against the wall and gazing over to Pier Head, across the grey water. The ferryboat was just leaving Liverpool to come over to us. I could see the Liver Birds, the carved birds on the top of the dark, brooding Liver Building.

'Someone said that if those birds ever fly away Liverpool will cease to exist,' I said.

Jean laughed. 'It had better not. I like Liverpool. When I'm grown up I'm going to live

there.' She said her favourite thing in Liverpool was the leccy, the overhead railway that ran on steel girders high above the ground along the dockside.

'Yeh, mine too. I like to watch the dockers heaving boxes and sacks on board ships that go all over the world.'

There was a strong breeze coming across the water and the wall felt cold and hard underneath me. I turned up my collar and sat on my hands.

'I wish Victor and Billy got on better,' Jean said.

'So do I.' I told her what Mam had said to me the day before, about how she thought Victor was suffering from delayed shock.

'What's that?'

'I'm not sure, but he's been more upset by the move than he's let on.' I remembered how I'd cried after the bomb landed on our old house, but Victor hadn't shown his feelings at all. He'd been too busy trying to help with things.

'Our kid has tried being nice to him,' Jean began.

'When?' I asked, jumping down from the wall. 'When was Billy nice to Victor?'

'He took him to the stables, didn't he?'

'And threw a bale of straw at him.'

Now Jean jumped off the wall and turned to face me. 'He didn't throw it at him. He threw it down.'

'And called him names,' I said.

'Oh, don't be so stupid,' Jean snapped back. But I wasn't stupid. I was feeling sorry for Victor now, and wanted to stick up for him. He was my brother!

'Your Billy goes on about his work all the time. He's a show-off. You said so yourself, so there.'

'You like him though, don't you?' said Jean. Her voice was quieter now. 'I've seen you looking at him. It's "yes Billy, no Billy".'

I ran at her, then stopped. 'Oh, don't let's quarrel over them. Lads are stupid. They're either fighting or showing off, most of 'em.'

'And thinking they're better than girls,' said Jean. 'Look, that ferry is nearly here.' I looked around at the darkening sky, full of black smoke from all the chimneys.

'Let's go.'

# CHAPTER 5

The next morning I was looking at the newspaper when the postman came to the door. I saw him hand Mam a small package.

'Dad! It's from Dad,' I screeched, dropping the newspaper. I recognised the stamps on the envelope – special ones for people in the forces. Mam tore open the package. There was a letter for each of us and a small packet of peppermints for me. I read my letter twice.

*Dear Sheila,*

*I miss you, love, and hope you're well. How's school? ...* I rushed on to the best bit. *I hope to be home soon for a couple of days.* He'd underlined the word *soon*.

'Yes!' He felt much closer already. I threw the letter in the air. 'Yes, yes, Dad's coming home!' Perhaps he was back in Britain already. Mam said they sometimes had to wait ages for trains home.

Victor opened his letter and out fell a big piece of silk.

'Parachute silk,' said Mam in amazement. Victor's mouth fell open. His eyes went wide and he started to jump up and down. I'd not seen him so happy for weeks.

'I can't believe it! Where did he get it?' He picked up the letter. 'Says a chap gave it him. Came from a beach in France.' He ran round the room waving the cream silk like a flag.

'It could be from when the Germans invaded France,' said Mam. 'You remember hearing all about our ships going out to Dunkirk to fetch our soldiers home from the beaches back in May.' She sounded as excited as Victor. 'You'll be the envy of the street, my lad. You'll see.'

I nipped over the fence to tell Jean about Dad's letter. We went for a walk round the block and ended up in the nearby timber yard, which smelled strongly of sawdust. A girl from our class was scrambling up a pile of planks. 'Can't catch me, I'm the wood yard flea,' she called out. The game turned into 'follow my leader', and she led us out of the smelly yard, waddling and clucking like hens with our elbows and bums sticking out. We stopped by the street gas lamp, laughing, just as Billy and some other boys came running down the street, pushing and shoving and trying to kick a stone. They lunged into us.

'Mind, stupid,' cried Jean. She picked up the stone and threw it over a wall.

'Aw, meany, meany,' they shouted.

Jimmy Wilson, who still had a plaster on his nose, leaned against the lamp-post and pulled a copy of *The Boy's Own Paper* out of his pocket. He turned to a page where there was a picture of a torpedo. We all clamoured to see.

'Look at that!'

'Cor, it says they travel just under the surface of the water at thirty-six miles per hour.'

'Cripes, that's as fast as a car!'

'*And* they can smash a boat five miles away.'

'Wow.'

'My dad says it's those German U-boats with their torpedoes we've got to sort out,' said Billy. 'They go underwater, searching for our ships, and when they find one – POW!' He smacked a fist into the palm of his other hand. 'We're gonna win the war, though, my dad reckons. He says now we've got Winston Churchill as prime minister we'll soon have those Jerries licked.'

'Never mind all that, look at this,' said another boy, opening his hand. We all peered down.

'Blimey!' In his palm lay a brass nose cone from a bombshell.

'You lucky so-and-so.'

The boys began getting their latest pieces of shrapnel and spent bullets from their pockets. It was getting dark. I knew I ought to go home. I looked up and saw Victor walking towards us. He'd left it a bit late, but I was suddenly pleased for him.

'You wait and see what my brother's got,' I said, proudly. 'It'll take your breath away!' Victor pulled the parachute silk from his pocket. There was a stunned silence, and then everyone began talking at once.

'Gosh, that's terrific, Vic.'

'I wonder what happened to the paratrooper?'

'Could be dead.'

'Could be captured – he could be a prisoner of war, or maybe the Allies found him.'

Billy reached for the silk. 'Let me look.' He tugged at the cream material in Victor's hand. 'Come on, scaredy cat, I won't steal it.' Victor let go. Billy looked closely at the silk, then waved it in the air and ran down the street. It billowed out behind him.

'Give it back,' cried Victor.

'Oh, don't be a spoilsport,' called Billy.

It was too late for games, but everyone got caught up in the excitement and ran after Billy, cheering and laughing. I caught up with Victor and grabbed his sleeve. 'I'm going home. Mam'll be worried. What if there's an air raid?' But I knew he wouldn't listen, and I knew I'd not leave him either.

Billy turned the corner into the street with the picture house. Suddenly the sirens went. Billy stopped dead. He let go of the parachute silk and the wind took it into the air.

'Stupid!' said Victor. He charged at Billy. Before you could say 'jump' they were sprawling on the ground, hitting each other.

I tried to pull Victor off Billy. 'Get up, the planes will be here. You'll be seen and shot.' But Victor wasn't listening.

'Just because you're jealous,' he snarled at Billy. 'My dad's in the war, fighting for his country, and yours isn't doing a thing.'

'That's not true!' Billy shouted. 'Dockers unload the ships. They bring us food. It's hard work, *and* my dad's an ARP warden, so there. He goes out to help people when there's air raids. He hardly gets any sleep some nights.'

'My dad's in the navy, though,' said Victor. 'They protect all the ships that come to the docks. *And* they risk getting torpedoed by the Germans. You've got to be brave to be in the navy.'

I thought Billy was going to punch him, but he didn't. 'My dad's as brave as yours,' he answered. 'The docks get bombed all the time.' I thought about the times I'd seen the walls of fire from the Liverpool docks, and the red skies above them.

I could hear the planes now, coming nearer and nearer. The searchlights were up. A plane hung silhouetted in one. The barrage balloons were waving menacingly like silver fish as the searchlights slid over them. All the other children had gone and the street was deserted.

Jean stuck her foot between the two boys, and yanked the back of Billy's jacket.

I poked Victor's back. 'There's your silk at the end of the street, it's come down.'

Billy and Victor broke up and hurtled towards it. The piece of parachute silk had landed in a dusty corner by a pub doorway. Billy grabbed it.

BANG! The noise silenced us all.

One street away, tiles and timber surged up into the air.

'Quick! Down there!' Billy pointed to an open trapdoor next to the pub. I could see a chute where deliverymen rolled beer barrels down into the cellar. Jean jumped down it. Billy followed her. It was my turn.

'HURRY. SHIFT YOURSELF!' said Victor behind me, and then he pushed me forward.

I shut my eyes and waited to land. It was pitch black in the cellar. I stumbled into Jean, then I bumped into a beer barrel. I could just

make out shapes of metal crates scattered all over the floor. I squeezed in between two crates.

I could hear voices and the sound of feet coming down steps into another room of the cellar.

'Told the wife I'd be home by eight,' one said. 'Fat chance of that now.'

Then the noise overhead got so loud I couldn't hear another word. I felt the building shudder and I cried out.

\*　　\*　　\*

We had to stay there for over an hour until the all-clear sounded. I stretched my cramped body. Men were walking up the stairs back into the pub. Victor climbed up the chute and tried to get the trapdoor open, but he couldn't. Billy tried, but it was no use.

A sudden beam from a torch arrowed into the room. We rushed towards it and looked up to see the blue uniform and steel hat of an ARP warden.

'DAD!'

'BILLY! What the heck are you doing down here? Stay where you are, there's a fire bomb up in the pub. I'll come and get you when it's safe.'

We could hear the squirting of a water pump as well as anxious voices calling instructions.

'More, more.'

'Here, over these flames.'

'Get sand.'

And then we heard the voices sink with relief. The bomb was out. Billy's dad reappeared at the top of the steps.

'Up you come, young 'uns.' We climbed the steps. The pub smelled of burned wood, and there was sand and grit everywhere.

'What on earth were you doing out so late, all of you?' Mr Adams looked cross and upset. 'You know the rules – in by seven at the very latest!' We hung our heads and said nothing.

Billy's dad walked us all home. Victor didn't say a word, but from time to time I saw him look across at Billy and his father, and bite his lip. The darkened streets, lit only by a few fires, were full of toppled buildings. Cars were hooting. Stray dogs were running around and I saw an RSPCA officer with a cat in his arms. One street was blocked by a fallen lamp-post and we had to go another way round to get to our street. I vowed I'd never stay out late again.

Mam was waiting for us at the back door. She heaved a huge sigh of relief and clutched me to her.

'Thank goodness you're safe,' she said.

She turned to Billy's dad. 'Thank you for looking after them, Mr Adams. Come in and have a cup of tea at least before you turn out again.'

'Eddie,' he said. 'Call me Eddie. Thanks, but I'd best go as I'm still on duty. The docks have copped it, I guess. It's getting as bad as London – it's constant daylight in the East End, they say. The Jerries seem to be giving us a real pasting now.'

As he left he turned. 'The raids were early tonight. It's not often they begin before nine o'clock. They caught everyone out.' I wasn't sure, but I thought he winked at me.

As Billy turned to go home, he stopped and fumbled in his pocket. He brought out the parachute silk. 'Here you are, Victor,' he said. 'It'll need ironing.'

# CHAPTER 6

Birkenhead had been badly damaged by the air raids. There'd been a second raid in the early hours of the morning. We'd all huddled in the cellar, me beside the coal heap and Victor near Mam, who sat on the stairs hugging her knees most of the time.

*    *    *

We slept until dinner time, and didn't go to school.

'Let's go look for souvenirs,' said Victor in the afternoon, 'and see what's happened down by the docks.'

'You be careful, the pair of you,' said Mam. 'Don't go anywhere that's cordoned off, promise me. I can't take any more after last night.' We promised.

*       *       *

'Blimey! What a mess!' We were coming out of Pig Snicket onto the main road. Houses and buildings were flattened. There was rubble everywhere and police and wardens were walking around with lists and notes trying to find missing people. The police station, which had been wrecked a few weeks ago, was still standing with a huge hole in its upstairs and sandbags piled high against the walls. But it looked neat compared with the new damage.

'There's twenty layers of sandbags on top of one another,' said Victor. 'I've counted them. Look – they go halfway up the ground-floor windows.' We walked on. Water swilled around where a pipe had burst. A warden saw us looking at it.

'Keep away,' he called, and held his arm out like a barrier. We didn't need a second telling.

It was even worse towards the docks. A bomb had ripped away a house wall, leaving the bath jutting out into nothingness. It was all cordoned

off but still didn't look safe.

'Come on,' I said. 'You can't go near any of this for souvenirs. It's too dangerous.' We headed towards the square, which looked to have escaped the bombing except for a partly demolished shop. 'And you won't find anything better than the parachute silk Dad sent.'

'I can't wait for Dad to come,' said Victor. 'Where do you think he is at this moment?'

'In England,' I said brightly.

'No, not yet, silly. He can't be.'

'Could be. He might …' I stopped. I grabbed Victor's sleeve. 'Hey! Look at that horse and cart over there.' The horse was struggling up a narrow street leading from the square. Sparks began flying from its hooves as they skidded on the cobblestones. 'Gosh, it looks like Billy!'

'It is Billy! Look, Toffee can't get a grip. CRIPES, they're running backwards. Come on!' He took my hand and we charged towards the horse and cart, scarcely looking across the road as we went.

'Billy!' I yelled from the bottom of the steep street. He'd jumped off the cart and was now pulling on Toffee's reins, but the horse was still sliding back. Toffee's head was jerking and Billy was tugging desperately. Victor grabbed the reins alongside Billy.

'Thanks,' shouted Billy. 'We've got to lighten the cart load.'

'I'll do that,' said Victor, 'you stay with Toffee', and quick as a flash he'd put a foot on a wheel and levered himself up onto the cart. I pulled on the reins with Billy, and all the time he was talking to Toffee.

'You're OK, boy. Gently now, gently.'

From up on the cart I could hear Victor groaning and panting. One sack thumped to the ground. Then another and another.

'Can you manage another couple?' Billy called.

'I'll try.' Victor's voice was strained with the effort. Sacks lay scattered all over the narrow pavement. Another sack hit the side of the road and burst, spilling white flour all over the place.

But Toffee was struggling less now. 'We're winning,' said Billy. 'I'm going round his back end to give him a push. You guide him gently round, Sheila, and the cart will follow. Then we'll get him back down the street into the square and to the stables.' He looked up at Victor again. 'Are you coming down?'

'No, I'll stay here and try and spread the sacks to even the weight.'

Billy and I began leading Toffee round. He was almost round when … FLASH! BOOM! My hands flew to my ears. A cloud of rubble and dust shot in the air from where the half shop had been. Through the haze I saw a wall slide into the ground. THUMP! The ground shook. Toffee lunged forwards, but the cart jolted, twisted and hit the lamp-post. Toffee was now wedged against the lamp-post, anchored by the cart. Sweating and frothing on his neck and shoulders, he bared his teeth in fear, and his eyes shone glassy white.

Victor was rolling on the floor of the cart, his cheek grazed and bleeding. Billy was hanging on as hard as he could to Toffee's reins. He was winding them round the lamp-post. Victor sprang up, and helped him tie them there.

'Oh crikey,' said Billy, letting out his breath. He leaned his head against the horse's damp shoulder. 'That must have been an unexploded bomb which just went off, Toffee. That's all. Don't worry, it's not near you.' He was talking to the

animal as though it was human. Toffee seemed to calm down a little. He stopped snorting, though his eyes were still wild. Down in the square police cars and fire engines screamed around, and the place was suddenly full of noisy people, wardens with whistles, and people cordoning off the area. An ambulance zoomed into the scene, and then another one.

'There might be another bomb,' said Billy. 'They often have delayed fuses. You go. Go on.'

'What are you going to do?'

'I can't leave Toffee.'

'You'll have to.'

'I'm staying. You go. GO!'

'Then I'm staying,' I yelled back.

'Me too,' said Victor.

Billy shrugged but he looked pleased.

'OK, I've got to get Toffee out of the shafts and then get the cart in the right position so I can tether him to the iron bar at the back of it. He should feel safer there and calm down a bit. Watch out for his feet.'

Toffee was still sweating and his eyes were rolling. Billy reached up and put his coat over Toffee's head, hoping the darkness would calm him. 'You're safe, my beautiful boy,' he whispered. 'Billy will put you round the back of your cart and then you'll feel better.'

Water hoses straggled across the pavement now, and firemen were up ladders spraying a fire. Toffee was kicking out.

'Keep away from him, Sheila,' Billy said. But I remembered what he'd told me at the stables, about how important it was to talk to, and touch, a frightened horse. I climbed onto the sand box, next to the lamp-post, so I could reach forward and stroke Toffee's back. And then I remembered the last of Dad's mints I'd been saving in my pocket. I knew that horses loved peppermint more than anything else. Whilst the boys undid the cart and put chains on its wheels, to stop it moving, I fished my last precious mint from my pocket and held it out to Toffee. He smelled it and in a second I felt his lovely soft nose snuffle over the peppermint in the palm of my hand. Then, while he crunched it, the three of us managed to get him tethered to the back of the cart.

'He's as safe as he can be,' said Billy. 'Now let's get out of here. Go on, Sheila.'

I ran down the hill. But when I turned round

neither Billy nor Victor were behind me. They were still with Toffee and I knew Billy would never leave the horse. I had to do something. They were cordoning off a huge area of the square. I remembered the man with the cat in his arms. I would find an RSPCA officer. They'd know what to do with Toffee. I ran on. I ran into the arms of an ARP warden, dodged quickly but found myself grabbed by a policeman.

'Get out of the area, child,' he shouted, 'or get into that shelter.' He pointed. 'There could be more bombs.'

'I've got to find an RSPCA man,' I cried.

'No way, my girl!' He lifted me up. 'You'll get out of here if I have to carry you myself.' I struggled out of his arms. 'NOW,' he said, and at that moment another wall slithered to the ground, and a parked car got buried in its bricks.

I turned to go back to the boys and Toffee, but then stopped. They'd gone! All of them. Where were they? There was no one there, just the empty street littered with white flour and sacks. I was on my own.

# CHAPTER 7

I ran up to the top of the street, but there was no sign of them. My heart was thumping like it was trying to jump out of me. Could they be going back to the stables some other way? That seemed likely. I carried on, not sure of the way there, but hurrying in the right direction. I got a stitch in my side and doubled up, in the doorway of a boarded-up house. This street was deserted. The windows of the houses had all been boarded up and the holes in the road still gaped, awaiting attention. It was a dismal, miserable sight, and it was starting to rain. I began to run again. I didn't stop until I got to the stables. I took a deep breath and walked in.

They were there, all three of them, talking to an RSPCA officer. I was too weak to shout out, but they rushed to me and Victor put his arms round me.

The officer was smiling. 'You did a splendid job between you,' he said. 'You probably saved Toffee's life and maybe other lives too. If horses bolt it almost always ends up in injuries.' I stroked Toffee's nose. He was in his box and quiet now. The officer patted my shoulder, rather like he patted the horses.

'Billy here tells me you were great with Toffee. You knew exactly what to do to calm him.'

'I remembered him telling me when he brought us to see Toffee,' I said, 'that's all.'

'He's had a small injection to calm him,' said Billy. 'He'll sleep.'

'Well, good luck with everything,' said the officer. He patted me on the shoulder again, then left us to attend to other problems.

'I'm not leaving Toffee now,' said Billy, and he spread himself across some bales of hay beside the horse's box. I looked at the boys. Billy's clothing was ripped and his hair was matted. Victor had a huge bruise on his cheekbone. I felt tired. My legs seemed to have stopped working. I flopped down on the hay for a rest before going home.

*   *   *

I opened my eyes. Oh no! I shook Victor. 'It's ten past six!'

He sat up, rubbing his eyes. 'We've been here for hours. What will Mam say?'

Billy opened his eyes and yawned. 'I'd better look at Toffee,' he said. He stood up, then turned to us, biting his lip. 'Thanks. Both of you. I couldn't have saved Toffee without you.'

A sudden coughing noise outside made us all look up. There was a sound of footsteps. Then the door opened and a shaft of light arrowed in.

'It's Dad!' I yelled. 'Dad! Dad!'

I ran and hurled myself into his arms, and hung round his neck, kissing him. He smelled clean and soapy and wonderful. Victor squeezed in, too, stretching his arms round both of us.

'Mam said you'd be here. An RSPCA officer told her you saved a horse's life or something.' We stayed in a huddle for what seemed ages, and then Dad moved forward to shake hands with Billy, who had already begun to tell him what had happened.

*   *   *

The next few days were some of the happiest of my childhood, despite the war. Dad had a 72-hour leave, which was supposed to be a long leave, but didn't feel like it. The day before he went back we had a party at our house. Mam said it was just a bit of a fancy tea but she'd asked the Adamses round, and there was the tin of salmon she'd been saving for a special occasion, and some dark gingerbread which she'd made from a wartime recipe leaflet. I've never seen Victor eat like he did that day. And guess what? Mam produced my party dress. She'd been working on it in the evenings when I was in bed. It was gorgeous, made of pale blue silky stuff. I wore it all day.

During my third piece of the gingerbread there came a knock at the front door. I'd almost forgotten we had a front door, for we hardly used it.

'We've got a surprise for you,' said Dad, laughing. None of the adults moved, but we kids did. On the doorstep stood Toffee, and beside him the RSPCA officer. Toffee was in all his finery. His horse-brasses shone. He had flowers woven into his harness, and his tail was done up fancy. It was plaited with ribbons in it.

'He's come to say thank you,' said the officer. As soon as Toffee saw Billy he pushed his head into the doorway, then he put one of his front legs over the entrance.

'He's coming in,' said Mam. And he did. He stood in the doorway and none of the adults stopped him. It was a sight I shall never forget for the rest of my life.

# EPILOGUE (1948)

There were no more arguments between Billy and Victor. But the war got worse. Almost every night those German planes attacked. Schools were closed. Before Christmas our Mams decided to have us evacuated. We all went to the same place. In Wales it was. Mam never stopped worrying about us, but as she said after the war, 'I always felt you were safer as a foursome.' And we worried about them, but luckily – and Mam would cross herself and look upwards whenever she said this – luckily we all survived.

Billy left school early, before the war ended, and got taken on by Atkinson's. Billy drives Toffee now. He loves every minute of the day with the horses, he says. And Jean, well she's just got a flat. Guess where? Liverpool! I'm going to college there in September, so I'm going to share with her.

The boys, or 'young men' as Mam calls them, have stayed friends. Billy still reminds Victor that he never did get his ollies back, but I reckon it's fair because Victor gave him a whole set of cigarette cards, ones with horses on, and I know he'll never part with those.

# GLOSSARY

**Air-Raid Precautions (ARP) wardens:** Men or women who helped during air raids by dealing with fire bombs, giving messages, helping people and keeping records.

**air-raid shelters:** Places where people went to be safe during an air raid. People built brick or steel shelters in their gardens. Many public shelters were built underground.

**air-raid siren:** A siren that warned that an air raid was about to happen, so people knew to shelter.

**all-clear:** A siren that sounded at the end of an air raid to let people know the raid was over.

**blackout curtains:** Curtains made of thick black material, which cut out all the light from windows. They were designed to prevent German bombers seeing where to drop their bombs.

**cigarette cards:** Cards enclosed in packets of cigarettes, which both children and adults collected. The cards were in series such as flowers or trains.

**Dunkirk:** In May 1940 the Germans attacked France, Britain's ally. Many British boats went over to save our soldiers from the beaches of Dunkirk and bring them back home.

**fire bomb:** A small, stick-like bomb that set things on fire when it landed.

**gas mask:** A mask that covered the whole face, to stop the person breathing in gas. Gas masks were designed for use in a gas attack, but no such attacks took place in Britain during the Second World War.

**gramophone:** A record player that was wound up by hand and did not need electricity.

**Jerries:** A nickname for the Germans.

**lav:** A lavatory, or toilet. Many houses had a lav in a small brick building in their backyard or garden.

**rations:** Limited amounts of food and clothing, given to each person during the war to prevent the country running out of supplies.

**U-boats:** German submarines used in both the First and Second World Wars.

**Women's Voluntary Service (WVS) officers:** Women who helped the war effort in many ways, from raising money to moving people if their homes had been bombed or were in dangerous areas.